'TOONS FOR OUR TIMES

A Bloom County Book of Heavy Meadow Rump 'n Roll

'TOONS FOR OUR TIMES

A Bloom County Book of Heavy Meadow Rump 'n Roll

Berke Breathed

Little, Brown and Company · Boston · Toronto

RRD

*Published simultaneously in Canada
by Little, Brown & Company (Canada) Limited*

PRINTED IN THE UNITED STATES OF AMERICA

5

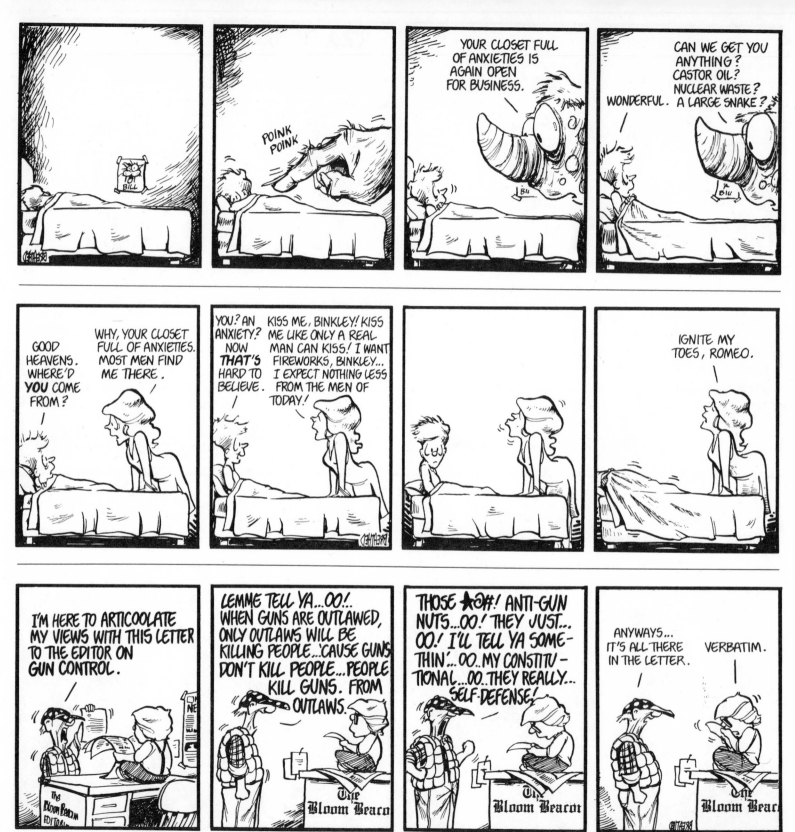

10

13

14

15

22

23

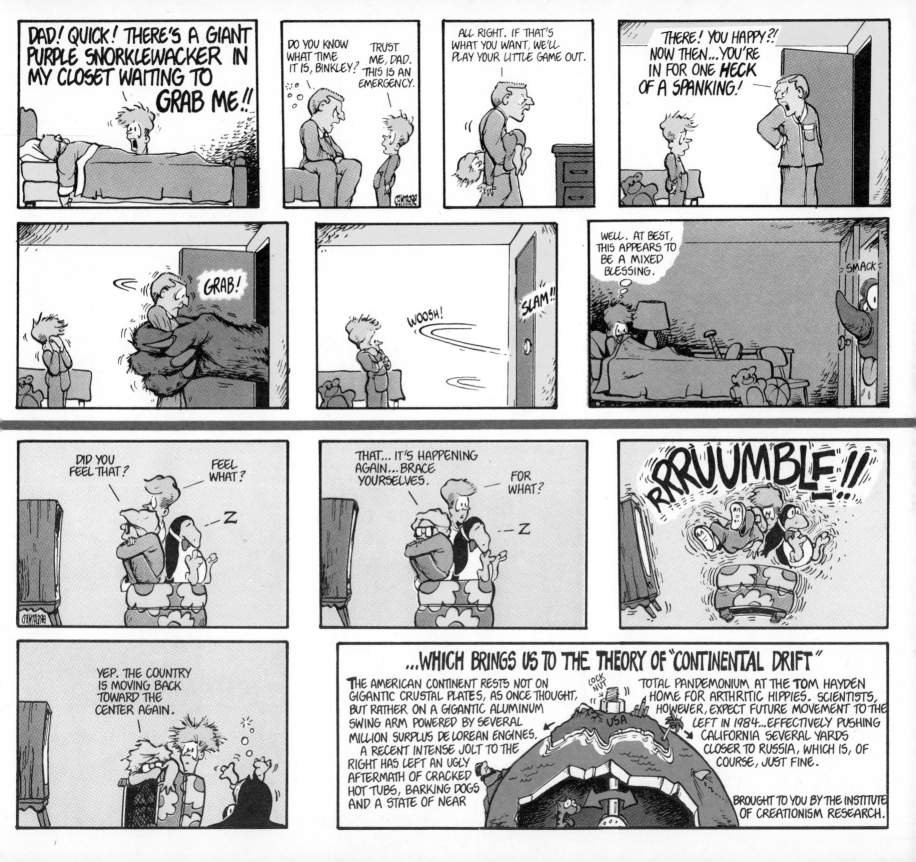

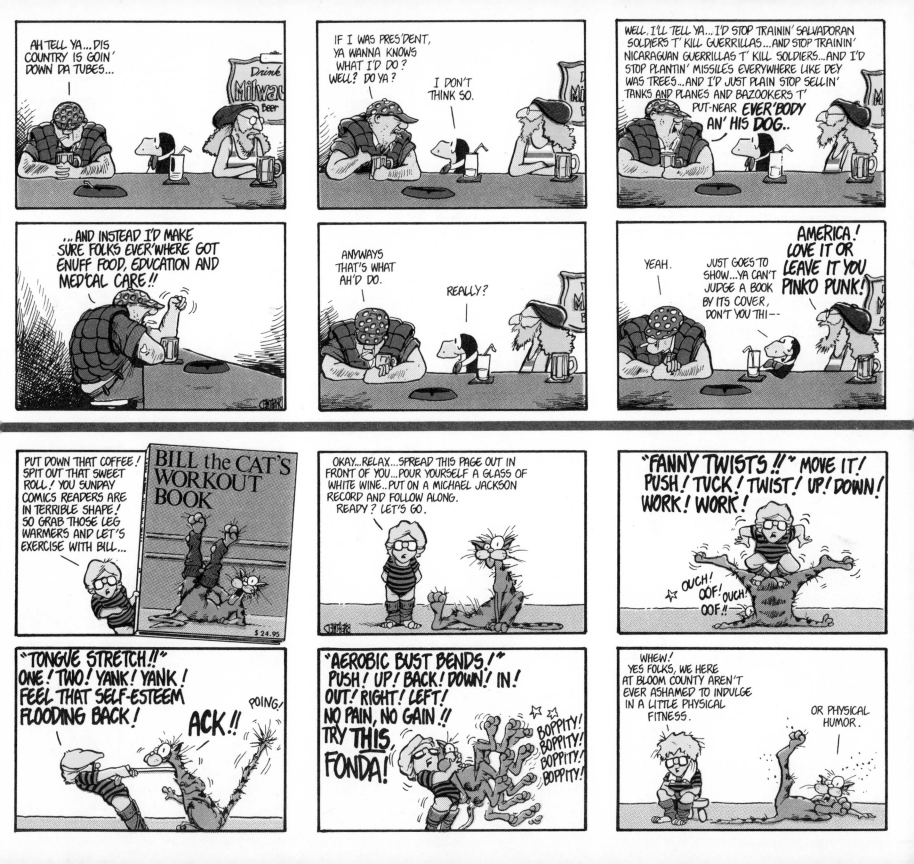

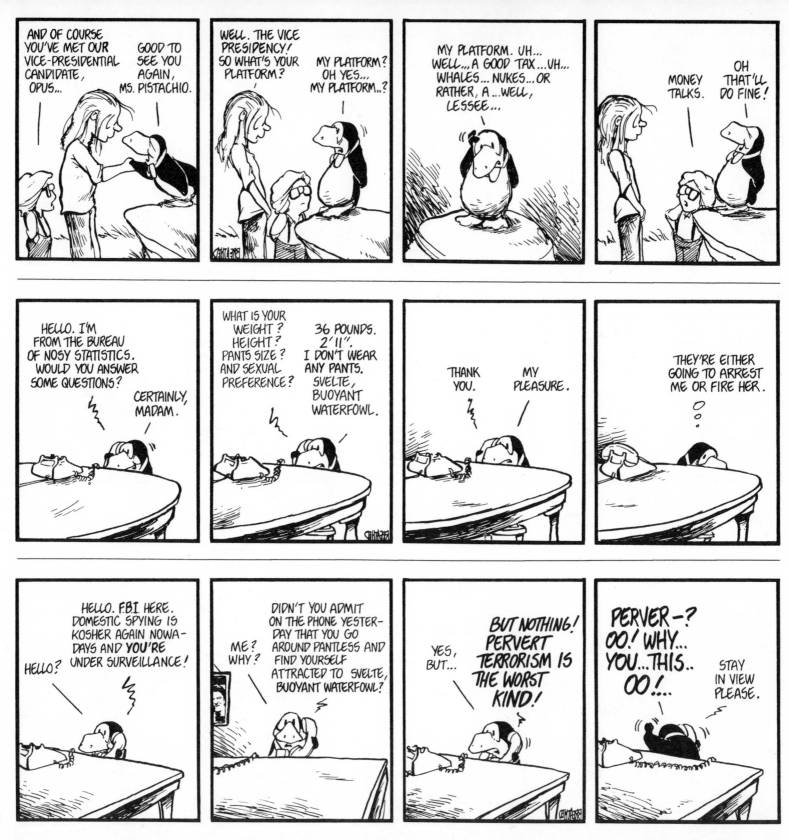

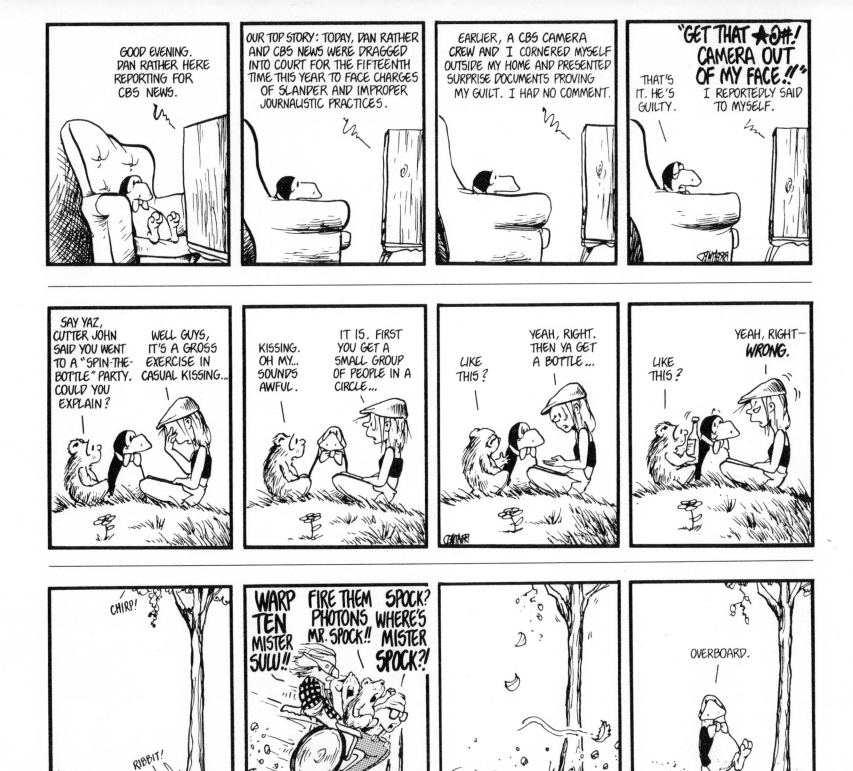

49

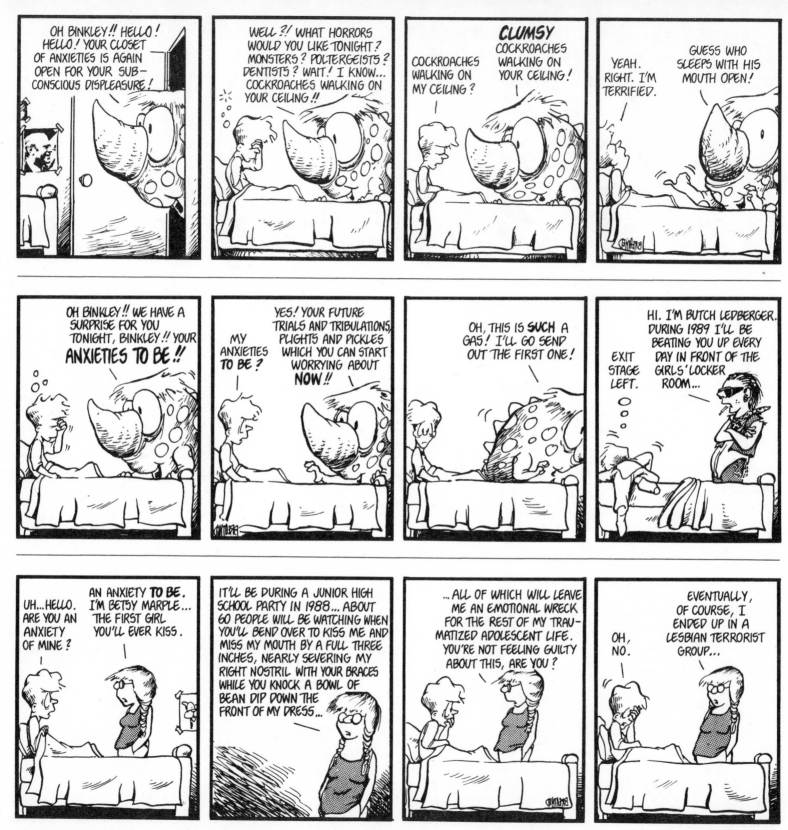

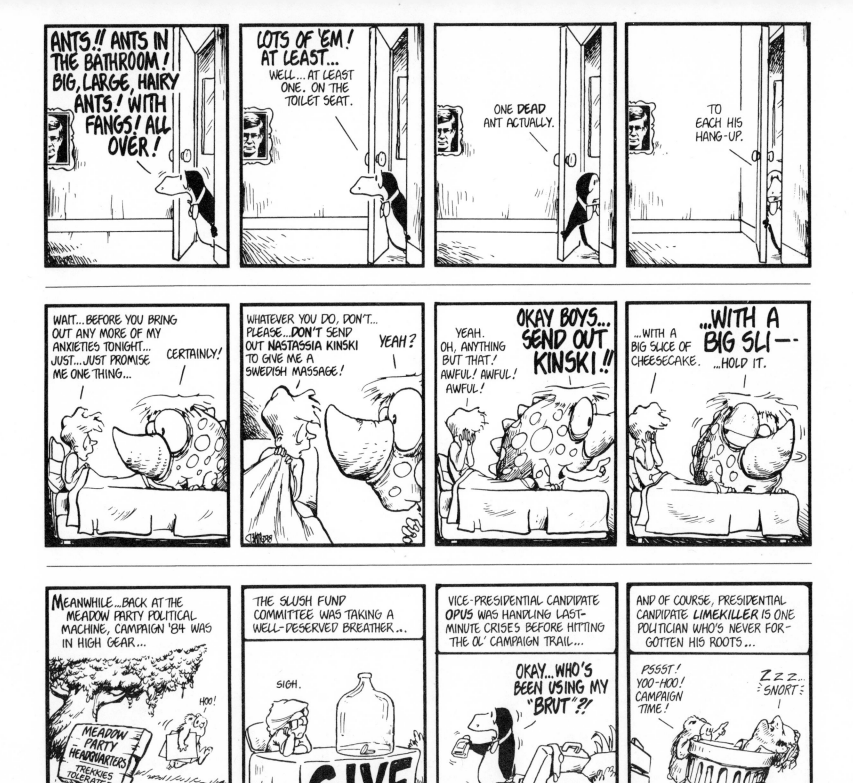

58

59

62

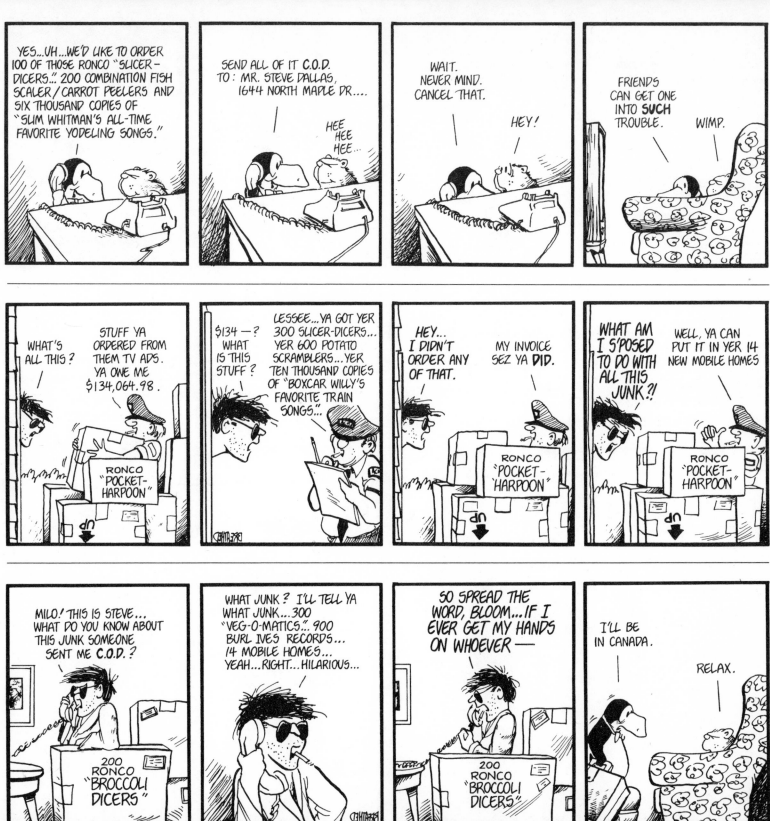

THE BILL THE CAT STORY

Part 1: The Early, Innocent Years

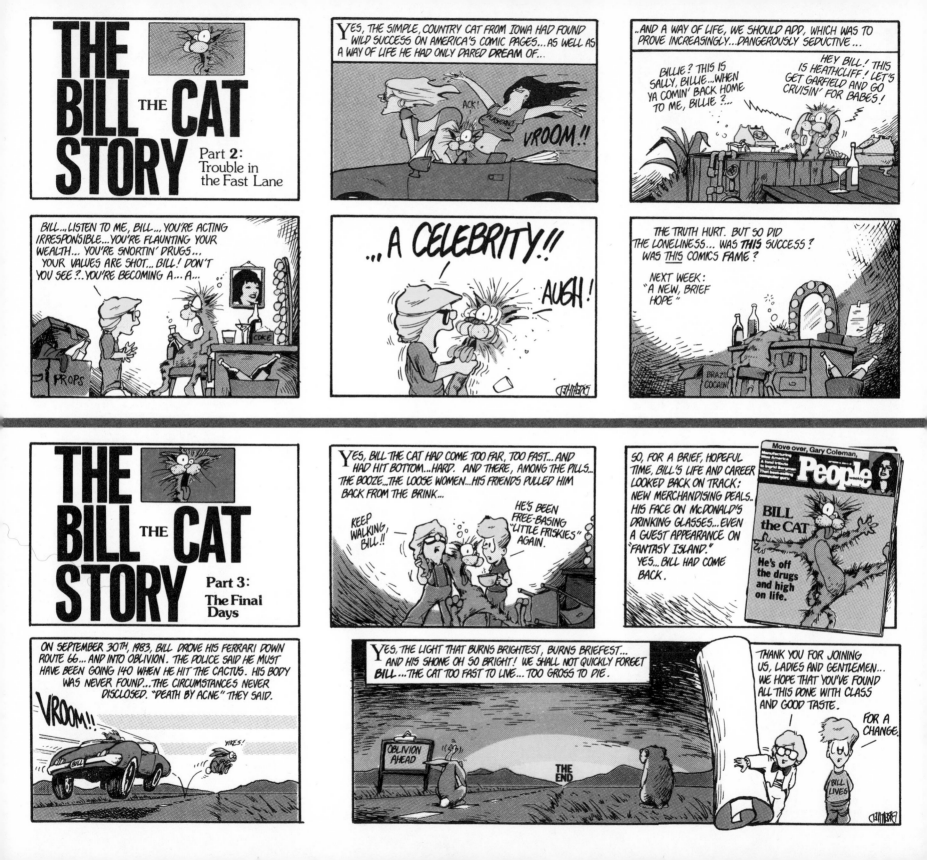

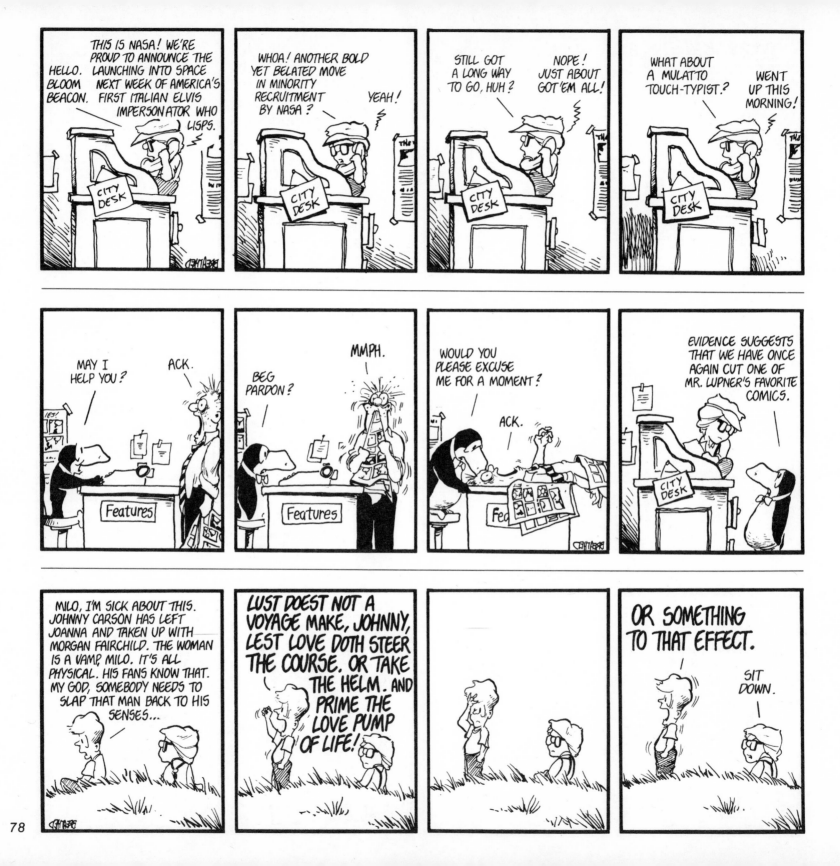

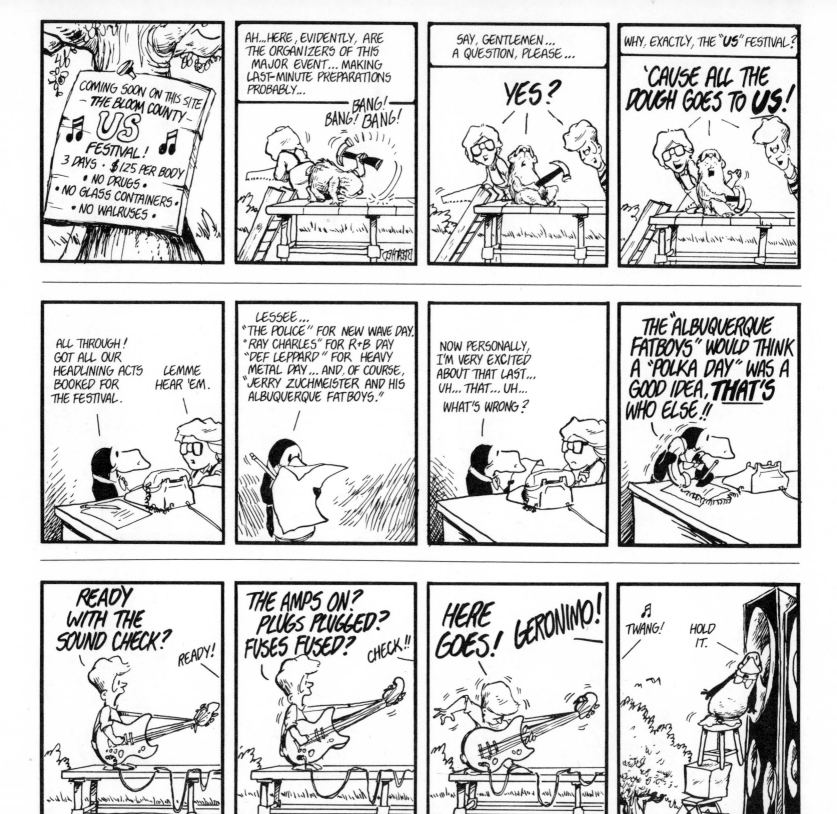

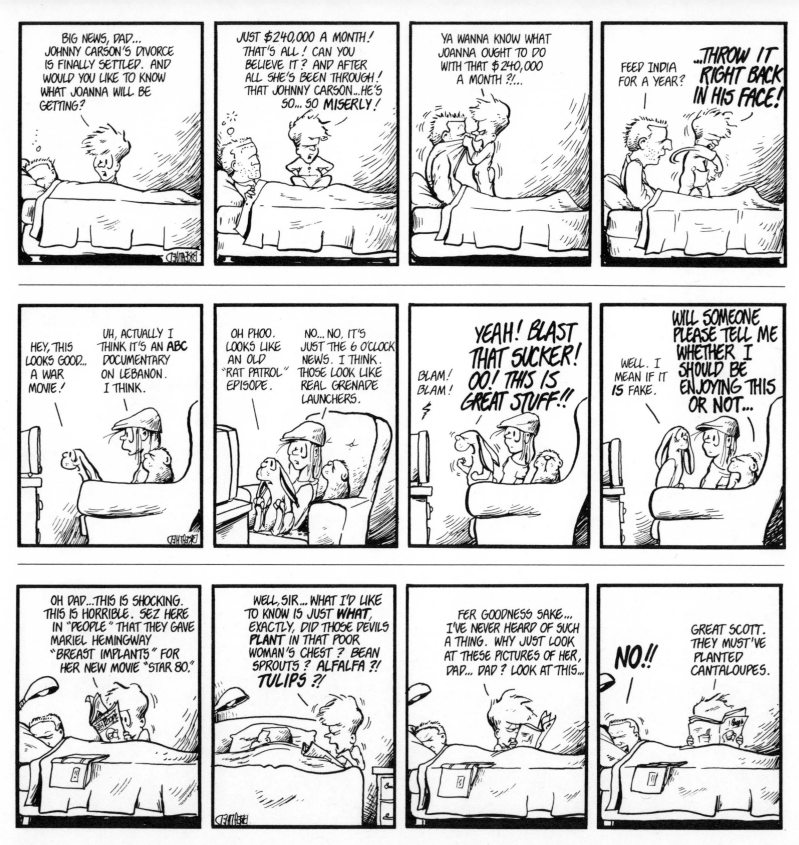

95